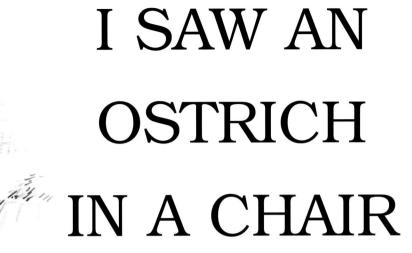

I SAW AN
OSTRICH
IN A CHAIR

(An Alphabet Book)

Dolores D. Goldich

Illustrations by Susan Weiss Baltic

STAR BOOKS

Star Books
I Saw an Ostrich in a Chair (An Alphabet Book)
Copyright © 2005 by Dolores D. Goldich
Illustrations by Susan Weiss Baltic

For further information, contact the author at:
DGoldich42@comcast.net

Book design by:
The Floating Gallery
www.thefloatinggallery.com

Dolores D. Goldich
I Saw an Ostrich in a Chair
(An Alphabet Book)

1. Author 2. Title 3. Children's Book

ISBN: 0-9762915-0-9
LCCN: 2004098331
Printed in China

To my dear husband and parents –   A a ALWAYS remembered
   my children and grandchildren –   B b the BEST
   my sister, who is –   C c so CLOSE.

    D.G.

To my mom and dad for their lifetime of love and support; to my husband and children for their patience and understanding; to my friends for their encouragement; and most of all to God for His gift of creativity.

    S.B.

Everybody! Come with me;

I saw some sights that you should see;

Down on the ground, up in the air,

You'll find surprises everywhere!

We take the alphabet all the way;

Please turn the page; we start with A....

A a

I saw an APPLE looking cross
'Cause it would soon be applesauce.

B b

I saw a BICYCLE cross the street;
An octopus sat on the seat.

C c

I saw a COAT of leaves today;
A strong wind blew the sleeves away.

D d

I saw a DOOR made out of cheese
With lots of holes just right for keys.

E e

I saw an ELEPHANT use its trunk
To raise a sailboat that had sunk.

F f

I saw a FAIRY wave her wand
To turn a puddle into a pond.

G g

I saw some GLASSES on a fish;
To see a mermaid was its wish.

H h

I saw a donut HOLE so big
That through it came a flying pig.

I i

I saw two melting cubes of ICE
With dots all over just like dice.

J j

I saw a JACK-IN-THE-BOX go POP!
And then show off with a big flip-flop.

K k

I saw some KETCHUP drip from the sun
On every thing and everyone.

L l

I saw a LUMP of purple clay
Turn into balls and bounce away.

M m

I saw a MONSTER drive a truck
In a traffic jam where he got stuck.

N n

I saw a NEEDLE cry and cry,
Then take a tissue and wipe its eye.

O o

I saw an OSTRICH in a chair;
Since it couldn't fly, it just sat there.

P p

I saw a PENCIL take a walk
With a crayon and a piece of chalk

Q q

I saw a QUILT on a lumpy bed;
A sleepy turtle poked out its head.

R r

I saw a RUG rise off the floor
And fly itself right out the door.

S s

I saw a SNOWMAN read at night;
The moon came out to give him light.

T t

I saw a TIE with stars of blue,
A birthday gift for a friend—guess who!

U u

I saw UMBRELLAS in the sky
Keeping birds and airplanes dry.

V v

I saw a VASE in a park near me;
Instead of flowers, it held a tree.

W w

I saw a WAGON pull a train
That pulled a bus that pulled a plane.

X x

I saw a XYLOPHONE and harp
Make music for a dancing carp.

Y y

I saw red YARN beside a kitten
Who was using it to knit a mitten.

Z z

I went to visit Dr. ZEE;
He checked my eyes; now look at me....

A a	APPLE	N n	NEEDLE
B b	BICYCLE	O o	OSTRICH
C c	COAT	P p	PENCIL
D d	DOOR	Q q	QUILT
E e	ELEPHANT	R r	RUG
F f	FAIRY	S s	SNOWMAN
G g	GLASSES	T t	TIE
H h	HOLE	U u	UMBRELLAS
I i	ICE	V v	VASE
J j	JACK-IN-THE-BOX	W w	WAGON
K k	KETCHUP	X x	XYLOPHONE
L l	LUMP	Y y	YARN
M m	MONSTER	Z z	ZEE